HALLOW'S EVE: THE CURSE OF THE BLOOD MOON

A YA GOTHIC FANTASY ROMANCE OF WITCHCRAFT, REBELLION, AND THE GIRL WHO CHOSE TO LIVE

ARIA BLAKE

Copyright © 2025 by Aria Blake

All rights reserved.

No part of this book may be reproduced in any form or by any electronic or mechanical means, including information storage and retrieval systems, without written permission from the author, except for the use of brief quotations in a book review.

CONTENTS

Part I
THE CHOSEN

1. The Harvest Festival — 3
2. Refuse the Call — 7
3. Unwelcome Legacy — 11
4. Threads of Rebellion — 16
5. The First Betrayal — 20

Part II
BLOOD BOUND

6. The Sleeping Witches — 25
7. The Binding — 29
8. Threads of the Moon — 33
9. Heart of the Curse — 37
10. The Plan — 41

Part III
BLOOD MOON RISING

11. Halloween — 47
12. Truth Undone — 50
13. One Must Die — 54
14. The Mourning Light — 58
15. Keeper of the Flame — 62

Afterword On Breaking the Cycle — 65

PART I

THE CHOSEN

1

THE HARVEST FESTIVAL

The fog rolled in just after dusk—low and thick like spilled milk, veiling the town in a silvery haze. It curled through the slats of fences, wound around lampposts, and clung to the ankles of festival-goers as they moved through the narrow streets of **Hallow's End**. The fog had a smell this year, Skye noticed. Not smoke, not cold—**something metallic**. Something ancient.

She stood at the edge of the square, the toe of her boot resting against the cobbled border where brick gave way to the blackened stage at the town center. Her breath fogged in front of her lips despite the unseasonably warm air. Around her, families laughed and twirled under lanterns strung between buildings, their yellow glow pulsing like candlelit stars.

This was supposed to be fun. It always had been. Skye remembered being a little girl, pulling a red velvet cape around her shoulders and pretending to be a witch as the Harvest Festival lit up the town for seven full nights—hayrides, mask parades, sugared nuts in paper cones, and the tradition everyone talked about but never really explained: **The Naming.**

This year was the hundredth anniversary. A centennial Blood Moon. And it showed.

Every storefront was dressed in exaggerated finery: lace-draped windows, skull-shaped lanterns, even the library had spelled its signage in Latin script for effect. The air hummed with expectancy. It wasn't joy—it was reverence.

And fear.

A flutter of red leaves swept across the square like bloodstained confetti, catching in the folds of Skye's jacket. She brushed them off and looked up. The moon was already high. Too high. Too red.

"Skye!" a voice cut through the haze.

Nova appeared, pushing through the crowd. Her black lipstick was smudged, and she was barefoot again—a habit Skye had long stopped trying to understand.

"Let me guess," Skye said as Nova approached. "You felt it, too."

Nova nodded grimly, her eyes reflecting the lantern light like a cat's. "The veil's thinner tonight. I saw a shadow walking beside me. No feet."

"You sure it wasn't just Elijah in another one of his awful cloaks?"

Nova didn't laugh. "I'm serious. It's starting."

Skye sighed, her gaze drifting toward the old church at the square's far end. Its steeple loomed like a knife in the fog, splitting the sky in two. Bells hung silent, but their weight felt oppressive.

Every hundred years, someone is Chosen.

It had always sounded like a myth. A folktale the town kept alive like nursery rhymes and old wives' curses. But this time... this time, the town felt different. And Skye couldn't shake the feeling that **she was being watched.**

Not by the crowd, not by the mayor or the cloaked elders who now stood whispering in a half-circle behind the dais—but by **something older.** Something with no shape, no name. It moved with the fog, threaded through the air like breath.

The music cut off with a sudden, discordant scrape.

Silence dropped like a veil.

The townspeople turned in unison toward the stage. There, Mayor Elswith climbed the steps with the slowness of someone stepping into sacred ground. Her long coat was buttoned up to the throat, its fabric catching in the wind like wings. She carried a small scroll bound in red wax.

Skye's pulse quickened. Her throat felt dry.

Elswith's voice echoed, clipped and cold. "As the Blood Moon rises on this centennial night, we gather to honor the pact made in blood and belief. We call upon the old names, the forgotten words, the guardians of our realm."

She paused.

"Tonight, we name the one who will walk between worlds."

The crowd shifted, quiet but not still. Some people reached for each other's hands. Others looked anywhere but the stage.

Skye tried to swallow. Her fingers clenched into fists inside her coat pockets.

The mayor held the scroll aloft. "This soul, freely given, shall preserve the boundaries of life and death. Light and shadow. The sacrifice is our protection."

She cracked the wax seal with a deliberate snap. Skye felt the tremor through the soles of her boots.

It wasn't possible.

It couldn't be—

"The Chosen of the Blood Moon is..."

A pause. The air itself froze.

"**Skye Amelia Mercer.**"

The world dropped out from under her.

No screams. No chaos. Just a silence so heavy it felt like drowning. Her ears rang with the echo of her own name, repeating over and over like a curse.

Skye didn't move.

She couldn't.

The crowd parted slowly, like a sea drawn back by an invisible tide. She felt eyes—dozens, hundreds—locking onto her. Some were full of pity. Others of awe. A few with something colder. **Relief.**

Nova reached for her. "Skye..."

But her voice was far away. Everything was far away.

The moon pulsed above them, red and full. And for a brief moment, just before she turned and ran, Skye could have sworn it was smiling.

2

REFUSE THE CALL

The Mercer house was quieter than usual.

No music played. No clinking glasses, no laughter echoing down the halls. Just the whisper of leaves against the windows, and the faint, metallic scrape of wind chimes swaying on the back porch. Skye stood in the entryway, arms folded tightly over her chest, as her mother lit a candle and placed it beneath the stained-glass window in the shape of a raven.

"A blessing," her mother murmured, smoothing her hands along her skirt. "A sacred honor."

Skye flinched. "Don't say that."

Her mother paused but didn't turn around. "Skye—"

"I'm not doing it," Skye snapped. "Whatever this is. Whatever *they* think this means. I'm not going to die for some old tradition."

Her father finally spoke from the kitchen doorway, voice low and tired. "No one is saying you have to die."

"Really?" she turned on him. "Because I'm pretty sure that's *exactly* what they're saying."

He looked away.

Skye stared at them both. "You knew this could happen. Didn't you?"

Neither of them answered. The silence told her everything.

Of course they knew. Of course they had hoped it would be someone else's daughter. Someone else's name on that scroll. That's what all the tight smiles and heavy glances meant over the past week. They had been waiting.

And now they expected her to *accept it.*

"I'm not a sacrifice," she said, her voice breaking. "I'm not."

Her mother finally turned, eyes shining with unshed tears. "You're not a sacrifice, Skye. You're... a symbol. The Chosen keeps the curse at bay. This town has survived a hundred years of peace because of this. Because of the pact."

"You mean the lie," Skye whispered. "Because that's what it is. Isn't it?"

The candle flickered violently, casting long shadows across the room. Her mother didn't answer.

SKYE SLAMMED her bedroom door and leaned against it, trying to breathe. Her heart felt like it was wrapped in thorns—too tight, too sharp. She couldn't think straight.

A soft knock.

"Skye?" Elijah's voice came through, muffled but careful.

She didn't answer at first. She wanted to be alone. But something in his tone—warm, steady, familiar—unraveled her.

She opened the door.

He stood there with his usual half-smile, but his eyes were shadowed. He held a thermos in one hand and a hoodie in the other. "Figured you might want something warm. And something to throw at me, if you're mad."

Skye almost smiled, but it didn't reach her eyes. "You heard?"

He stepped inside. "Everyone has."

They sat on the edge of her bed, the silence between them thick and heavy. He handed her the thermos—peppermint cocoa, her favorite—and she took a long sip, grateful for the warmth in her throat.

"Do you believe in it?" she asked after a while. "The curse?"

Elijah hesitated. "I believe in tradition. I believe in what the town *thinks* it knows."

"That's not an answer."

He looked down at his hands. "I don't want anything to happen to you."

There it was again—**the dodge**. A careful sidestep. He wasn't saying she'd be fine. He wasn't promising anything. He was avoiding it. And Elijah never avoided things. Not with her.

Skye narrowed her eyes. "What aren't you telling me?"

Elijah looked up, startled. "What?"

"You've been weird since the Naming. Since *before* it, actually. I thought you were just stressed about college stuff, but now..."

He opened his mouth. Closed it. Finally, he sighed. "It's not my place."

"You're my best friend. If something's going on, if you *know* something—"

"I can't," he said sharply. "I'm sorry, Skye. I can't."

She stared at him, stunned. The look on his face wasn't fear. It was guilt.

"Get out," she whispered.

Elijah didn't argue. He stood, lingered for a moment at the door, then left without another word.

LATER THAT NIGHT, Nova climbed through her bedroom window like she always did—quiet as breath and smelling like bonfire smoke.

"I brought you something," she said, tossing a bundle wrapped in velvet onto the bed.

Skye unwrapped it. Inside was a thin leather journal, brittle with age. Inked in swirling script across the first page: **Isolde Thorne**.

"Where did you get this?" Skye whispered.

"Old archives under the library," Nova said. "I've been digging. That 'sacred pact' they love to recite? It wasn't a gift. It was a warning."

Skye's blood chilled.

Nova sat beside her, voice low and urgent. "They don't tell us everything, Skye. They only tell us what keeps the story alive. But this—" she tapped the journal "—this tells another story. About the witches who built this town. About betrayal. About a curse made of blood and belief."

Skye looked at the moonlight seeping through her curtains, pale and cold. Her voice trembled.

"What if I don't believe in it anymore?"

Nova's eyes gleamed.

"Then maybe you can break it."

3

UNWELCOME LEGACY

THE WITCH AND THE FLAME

Hallow's End — 100 Years Ago
The flames licked the sky like hungry tongues, and the screaming had long since stopped.
Isolde Thorne stood tall in the center of the square, bound in iron that burned colder than fire. Her lips were split, her hands bloodied from struggle, but her eyes—her eyes were wild stars. Defiant.
Above her, the Blood Moon bled across the heavens.
"They say you would save us," whispered Mayor Halden, stepping close enough that ash clung to his boots. "But you would doom us all."
"I would free you," Isolde rasped. "You're too afraid to see the difference."
Children watched from behind their mothers' skirts. Elders chanted the Rite of Sealing. And the Watchers—their black cloaks still, their faces masked—tightened the circle around her. In their hands, they held the bloodstone.

> "The pact is made," Halden said. "The curse will protect what you tried to unravel."
> "You bind yourselves to death," she spat. "A town built on sacrifice will drown in silence."
> And then she screamed—not from the fire, not from fear, but in fury. A cry that split the veil and echoed into time itself.
> The moon turned crimson.
> The curse was sealed.

∼

Present Day – Three Days After the Naming

Skye had always liked storms. The way they shifted the sky into something wilder. The way the world seemed to hold its breath before thunder cracked it open.

But this storm wasn't in the sky. It was in her blood.

It had been three nights since the Harvest Festival, and Skye had barely slept. Not because she didn't want to, but because every time she closed her eyes, she *saw things*. Fractured, fevered visions that felt less like dreams and more like memories. Like someone else's life leaking into hers.

Witches burning.

A woman screaming her name from within a circle of flame.

Children dancing in a ring under the Blood Moon, chanting in a language she didn't recognize.

And then, always—**the Moon**, crimson and full, swelling in the sky like an open wound. Closer each time. Closer still.

She'd started sleeping with the window locked and her curtains drawn, but it didn't help. The light found her anyway, slipping beneath her eyelids like blood beneath a door.

She was unraveling.

THAT MORNING, Skye skipped school. Her parents didn't even question it. Her mother had taken to leaving bowls of salted water by every door. Her father walked around muttering old protection rites under his breath. Neither of them looked her in the eye.

In the suffocating quiet of the house, she wandered—slow and aimless, until her feet led her to the attic.

The door had been closed for years. Ever since her grandmother died.

It groaned when she opened it, the sound long and slow, like something waking up. Dust motes danced in the slanting sunlight, the air tinged with cedar, old perfume, and time.

She climbed carefully, fingers grazing the wall for balance, her heart pounding for reasons she didn't fully understand.

The attic was cluttered with forgotten things. Old trunks. An antique rocking chair. Her grandmother's full-length mirror, now cracked straight down the center.

But it was the trunk beneath the round stained-glass window that called to her.

She didn't know how long she stood staring at it. Long enough for the shadows to shift. For the air to still.

The iron latches were cold, etched with symbols she didn't recognize—one looked like a crescent moon tangled in thorned vines.

The lid creaked open, and the scent hit her first—old paper, lavender, and something deeper, almost metallic.

Inside, layered between yellowed lace and crumbling letters, was a leather-bound book. The cover was blackened and cracked, embossed with a symbol that made her breath catch.

A rose wrapped in thorns beneath a crescent moon.

She had seen that before.

On her grandmother's gravestone.

She lifted the book with trembling fingers and opened it.

The first page was filled with looping, elegant script, faded but legible:

This grimoire belongs to Isolde Thorne. Daughter of fire. Breaker of bonds. The Fifth.

Skye sat back hard, heart pounding.

Isolde.

The same name Nova had whispered after the Naming. The same name that had haunted her dreams for three nights straight.

She flipped through the pages. Spells written in a language she didn't understand. Drawings of moons in different phases, each with annotations. Instructions for rituals. Blood sigils. A warning scrawled along the margin in dark red ink:

If the bloodline is awakened, the Moon will call her back.

Skye slammed the book shut, breath ragged.

THAT NIGHT, the dreams returned.

She stood in a forest of blackened trees, their trunks split and burning. The air smelled of ash and salt. Voices whispered from behind the trunks, too low to understand. She turned—and saw her.

A woman with wild black curls, skin scorched at the edges, her dress torn and soaked in red. Her eyes were a storm.

She stepped forward, raising a hand toward Skye.

"Blood calls to blood," she whispered. "You are mine."

Then flames erupted at her feet.

Skye woke screaming.

SHE SAT at her desk in the pale light of dawn, the grimoire open in front of her, a cup of untouched tea cooling at her elbow.

She didn't know how long she'd been sitting there when Nova appeared.

She climbed through the window like she always did, dressed in mismatched layers and eyes full of fire. She tossed her bag onto the floor and dropped into the chair opposite Skye.

"I found her," she said without preamble. "Or at least... what's left of her."

Skye blinked. "Who?"

"Isolde Thorne," Nova said, pulling out a crumpled packet of notes. "She's not just some legend. She was *real*. One of the founding witches of Hallow's End. But every record past the year 1925? Gone. Redacted. Replaced with the 'official' four."

Skye's voice was hoarse. "Why?"

Nova looked at her grimly. "Because she rebelled. She was against the pact. She tried to destroy it. Said it bound the town to something darker than they understood."

Skye's eyes flicked to the book between them.

"She's my ancestor," she said quietly. "This was hers."

Nova stared at the cover, then back at Skye. "That's the Thorne seal. Your grandmother must've kept it hidden."

"I keep seeing her," Skye whispered. "In dreams. In flames. She says... I belong to her."

Nova leaned in, voice low. "Then maybe she's trying to warn you."

Skye looked down at the grimoire. At her name, scrawled in pencil beneath Isolde's—someone had added it later.

Skye Amelia Mercer.

And underneath it, in unfamiliar, looping script: *"The last Thorne. The cursed heir."*

Her hands shook as she closed the book.

She felt it now. Deep in her bones. The pull of something older than blood. The gravity of a destiny she didn't ask for—but could no longer deny.

The Moon had chosen her.

But she was done being chosen.

4

THREADS OF REBELLION

Four Nights After the Naming
    The fog was thicker than usual.

Not drifting and dreamy like it had been before—but alive. Intentional. It clung to the trees like breath and bled through the woods like smoke from a fire that hadn't quite burned out. Skye pushed a branch out of her way and stepped into the clearing, boots squelching in the damp, moss-covered ground.

The forest at the edge of town had always felt strange. Untouched. Too quiet. Her grandmother used to call it the Hollowing Wood, though no one else used that name anymore.

Nova walked beside her, hood pulled over her hair, a satchel of chalk, salt, and dried herbs slung over one shoulder.

"You sure about this?" Nova asked, voice low. "The Elders would hang us from the chapel spire if they knew we were performing a ritual outside of sanctioned ground."

Skye gave a tight smile. "Let them try. They already picked me to die. What else are they going to do—kill me twice?"

Nova didn't laugh. She just kept walking.

. . .

The clearing was perfect.

Moonlight filtered through the canopy in pale streaks, glinting off dew-slick grass. The fog hovered just above the ground in slow-moving tendrils. It was like stepping into another realm—one older, quieter, and far more dangerous.

Skye laid the grimoire gently on a flat stone at the center. She flipped to the page Nova had marked—titled *The Calling of Lineage.* The ink shimmered faintly under the moonlight, like it was breathing.

Nova knelt and began drawing the circle: ash, salt, blood from a small cut on her palm. Skye watched in silence, her heartbeat a war drum in her ears.

"When did you know?" Skye asked. "That you were... connected?"

Nova paused. "I didn't. Not really. But I always felt different. Like I was born sideways. My mom used to say the Thorne line was dead. But she was lying. And now I know why."

"You're a Thorne too," Skye said softly.

Nova nodded. "We both are."

A bitter laugh escaped Skye's throat. "So that's why we're cursed? Because of who we're related to?"

"No," Nova said. "Because we're the ones who can *end it.*"

The ritual began with breath.

Skye knelt across from Nova, mirroring her posture. The grimoire sat between them, open wide, ink pulsing faintly in time with the rhythm of the woods—if the woods had a heart.

Nova began the chant. Her voice was clear, steady, speaking in a language that didn't belong to this world anymore.

Skye followed.

At first, it felt ridiculous. Then—dangerous. Then—*right.*

The wind shifted.

The fog pulled inward, folding itself into the circle like fingers curling into a fist. The candles flickered blue. The salt lines hissed.

Then the air went still.

Utter silence.

Then—

The flame in the center burst high, as if someone had thrown oil into it.

And she appeared.

Flickering, faint, like a candle seen through rain.

A woman in a dark, tattered gown. Her face was obscured by hair tangled like vines. Her eyes burned like coals, and yet—there was something familiar in them. Something that made Skye's spine lock and her heart stagger.

Isolde.

She stood just outside the circle, not quite real. Not quite gone.

Her voice was a whisper carried on wind and ash.

"My blood walks again."

Skye couldn't breathe. "What are you—why me? Why now?"

Isolde tilted her head.

"Because the curse remembers. And so does the Moon. You carry what I could not destroy."

Nova stepped forward, voice trembling. "Can we stop it?"

The ghost's gaze snapped to her.

"You *must*. Or the next Blood Moon will never set."

Lightning cracked somewhere far off, and Isolde began to fade, her form unraveling into smoke.

Skye lunged forward. "Wait—! How?!"

But the spirit was already gone.

The circle burned itself into the earth.

The clearing fell dark.

Only the grimoire remained—open to a new page that hadn't been there before.

Its title:

The Moon Demands Blood.

SKYE STARED AT THE WORDS, her voice hollow. "She didn't just want to break the curse."

Nova looked at her. "No. She wanted to end the source."

Skye turned her face toward the sky.
The Blood Moon was rising again—earlier than it should have.
The clock was speeding up.
And now, she wasn't just running from destiny.
She was running out of time.

5

THE FIRST BETRAYAL

Skye hadn't spoken to Elijah since the ritual in the forest.

She'd meant to call him, maybe even apologize for snapping at him days ago—but ever since Isolde had flickered into existence and whispered *you carry what I could not destroy*, Skye's world had cracked wide open.

There was no space for apologies anymore.

Only war.

It was past midnight when she slipped out of the house. Nova was asleep—or pretending to be—in the guest room downstairs. The town square was empty except for leaves skittering across stone and the ever-present hush that had fallen over Hallow's End since the Naming.

Skye moved like a shadow, hugging the edges of buildings, careful with her steps. Something about the air tonight buzzed against her skin. The feeling of being watched had become a constant presence. She no longer knew if it was paranoia or prophecy.

She didn't expect to find Elijah.

But there he was—standing just inside the chapel garden, beneath the twisted yew trees where the Watchers were once buried. He wasn't alone.

Skye slipped behind a statue, holding her breath as she listened.

"—She's getting too close," said a voice she recognized: Elder Rowan, head of the town's founding family.

"She found the grimoire," Elijah replied. His voice was low, strained. "And the Thorne bloodline has awakened."

"So you know what must be done."

A pause.

Then Elijah: "I can keep her compliant until the ceremony. She trusts me."

The words sliced through Skye like a knife.

She didn't wait to hear more. She was already moving—fast, quiet, half-blind with fury.

BACK IN HER ROOM, she slammed the window shut and sank to the floor, breath shaking, hands trembling with rage and disbelief.

He was one of them.

A **Watcher**.

Sworn to the Order. Sworn to protect the curse.

And she had trusted him with everything.

> 🗝 **Journal Excerpt — Isolde Thorne**
> Dated October 28, 1925
> He walks beside me with soft eyes and gentle lies. The Watchers always smile before they strike.
> They were once protectors, but the blood moon made them cowards. They would sooner sacrifice the innocent than risk their power.
> One of them swore he loved me. And perhaps, in some small way, he did.
> But love does not silence screams. Love does not bind wrists to flame.

. . .

The next day, Elijah came to her.

He climbed through the window like he always had since they were kids, brushing leaves from his jacket.

"Skye," he said, voice soft. "I needed to see you. Talk to you. I know things have been—"

"Shut up."

He blinked. "What?"

She stood. "How long?"

He swallowed. "I don't—"

"How long have you been lying to me, Elijah?"

Silence.

"Since we were ten?" she snapped. "Since you gave me that carved moonstone and told me you'd always protect me?"

"I *am* protecting you—"

"No, you're protecting *them.*" Her voice broke. "You stood there and told them I trusted you. That you'd keep me in line until they murdered me."

He stepped toward her, but she backed away.

"I didn't want this," he said, voice raw. "I never wanted to be a Watcher. I was born into it. Just like you were born into the curse."

"So that makes it okay?" she whispered. "You were supposed to be my escape. Not my cage."

He looked like she'd hit him.

"Skye... I love you."

"No," she said. "You loved the version of me who didn't know better. Who didn't fight back."

She turned away. "We're done."

Outside, the wind picked up. The air smelled like fire.

And somewhere beyond the veil, Isolde Thorne whispered:

"Let the betrayers burn."

PART II

BLOOD BOUND

6

THE SLEEPING WITCHES

The door beneath the chapel had no handle—only a symbol carved into the stone: a crescent moon crossed with thorns.

Nova ran her fingers across it, her breath clouding the cold air. "It's Thorne sigil-work. The old kind. Blood-activated."

Skye held up her hand. A cut still scabbed across her palm from the ritual in the forest.

"You think it'll work?" she whispered.

"Only one way to find out."

She pressed her hand to the stone.

At first—nothing.

Then, a soft *click*.

The stone pulsed faintly, like it remembered something, and a crack formed down the center of the door. Dust spilled out as it groaned open, revealing a staircase carved into the earth—spiraling down into blackness.

THEY MOVED SLOWLY, Nova lighting the way with a charm stitched into her palm—an ember glow that barely touched the walls. The air was thick, not with decay, but **memory**—as if the stone itself had been holding its breath for a century.

The deeper they went, the colder it became.

Skye brushed her fingers along the walls. Symbols were carved into the stone: old witch marks, some protective, others binding. One repeated over and over again like a warning: **Vita Ex Umbra.** Life from shadow.

"Where are we?" Skye asked softly.

"Where they buried everything they wanted forgotten," Nova murmured.

At the bottom of the staircase, the catacombs opened into a vaulted chamber—circular, vast, and cloaked in silence.

Stone archways lined the room like ribs. In the center stood a basin, dry now, but blackened at the edges. Skye stepped closer and saw it had once held blood. Not metaphorically. **Actual blood.**

Nova knelt at a cracked pedestal nearby. A rusted lock gave way beneath her touch, and a drawer slid open with a groan.

She pulled out a stack of parchment, wrapped in oilcloth.

"Town records," she said. "Older than the official ones."

Skye leaned over her shoulder as she unrolled them, and her breath caught.

There were names. Symbols. Maps.

And then—a page that showed five women in a circle beneath a blood-red moon. At the center, a name scrawled in darker ink than the rest: **Isolde Thorne.**

"They were trying to protect the town," Nova said slowly, "but not from war. Not from famine."

She flipped the page.

The next one was darker. The drawing showed a figure—towering, robed in shadows, its face hidden by bone. A spirit. A god. A *death-being*. At its feet, a woman knelt, offering something that looked like a heart.

"They made a deal," Nova whispered. "The Blood Moon Pact wasn't about prosperity. It was about protection—from *this*."

Skye stared at the figure. Its eyes were empty sockets, but she felt them watching her.

"They feared this death spirit," Nova said. "So the Founders sealed it—fed it one soul every hundred years to keep it asleep."

Skye backed away from the drawings. "So it's not a curse... it's a bribe."

"And Isolde?" Nova said. "She wanted to destroy the spirit. Not feed it."

A SOUND ECHOED BEHIND THEM.

Not footsteps—but *breathing*.

Nova stood, reaching for the sigil blade at her waist. Skye turned toward the darkened archway—heart thundering.

From the shadows, a figure emerged.

And another.

And another.

People—maybe a dozen—hooded and pale, like moonlight made human. But they didn't move like townsfolk. They didn't look like the descendants of Elders or Watchers. Their clothes were old-fashioned. Their eyes glinted with silver.

"We thought you might find us," said the tallest woman. Her voice was neither warm nor cruel. Simply resigned. "The Thorne line always returns."

Skye stepped forward. "Who are you?"

"Survivors," the woman said. "Descendants of those who followed Isolde. We were exiled when she fell. We hid. We've waited."

"For what?" Nova asked.

The woman's lips curled into something almost like a smile. "For the bloodline to awaken. For the seal to falter. For the Moon to rise... out of cycle."

Skye swallowed. "You know about the Blood Spirit."

"More than the Elders ever did. They gave it a name. A place to sleep. But they never understood what they chained."

"And now?" Skye whispered.

The woman stepped closer. Her eyes were the same pale gray as the fog that never left the woods. "Now it wakes."

A hush fell.

The woman turned, gesturing toward a door carved into the wall behind them—one that shimmered faintly, sealed with layers of magic.

"The answers you seek lie beyond," she said. "But answers have prices."

Skye met her gaze. "So does silence."

7

THE BINDING

PROLOGUE: THE FAILED BINDING

Hallow's End — October 30, 1925
The circle was incomplete.
Isolde knew it the moment she spoke the final word. Something in the air shuddered. A thread had snapped—too thin, too weak.
The others didn't see it. The Elders chanted. The fire burned.
*But the **Blood Spirit** did.*
It surged forward—not with a body, but a scream, like every soul ever lost had opened its mouth at once.
One of the other witches fell—Elira, the youngest. Blood spilled into the center of the ritual.
Isolde reached out to catch her, but it was too late.
The binding shattered.
The Moon turned black.
*And in its place, **red lightning forked through the heavens.***

Present day.

The exiled witches led Skye and Nova through the sealed door beneath the catacombs, into a chamber that felt like it had been carved from bone.

The stone here was smoother, colder, older. It pulsed faintly with buried sigils, and the air smelled not just of dust, but **iron**—as if magic itself had bled into the walls.

At the far end of the room stood a pedestal. Upon it sat a basin, etched with the five original founding marks—one of which Skye now recognized as the **Thorne seal**.

Nova touched the rim with reverence.

"They tried to bind it here," one of the witches said behind them. "Once. It failed."

Skye turned. "Why?"

"The Moon was too strong. The pact already made. They underestimated its hunger."

Nova looked down into the basin. "We won't."

The witch hesitated. "You carry Thorne blood. And hers." She nodded at Skye. "But even that might not be enough."

Skye looked at Nova. "We do it anyway."

THEY PREPARED IN SILENCE.

Skye poured a circle of salt and bone ash. Nova placed five obsidian shards at the cardinal points. The exiles watched without interfering, though their eyes glittered with something between hope and dread.

Nova opened the grimoire to the ritual.

Binding of Shadowed Flame: A Tethering Between Realms.

The spell required blood. Power. Intention. And unity.

Nova slit her palm without flinching.

Skye hesitated—but followed.

Their blood hit the basin at the same time. The air snapped.

Then—nothing.

For a heartbeat.

Then the fire in the torches along the walls **flared blue**.
And Nova screamed.

POWER POURED FROM HER—NOT graceful, not elegant, but wild and brutal and ancient. Her eyes rolled back. Her body lifted several inches off the ground, wind screaming through the chamber.

The ritual spiraled out of control.

The salt line *broke*.

Skye lunged forward, trying to hold the circle together with her hands, blood and bone searing into her skin. But the energy backlashed and **threw her across the chamber**, slamming her into the stone wall.

Everything blurred.

Sound fell away. Her lungs refused to pull air.

The Blood Moon was in her mind again—closer now. **So close.**

A whisper coiled through her head like smoke:

"You were born for this."

"Give in."

HANDS ON HER SHOULDERS.

Nova's voice, shaking. "Skye. Skye, stay with me—please, please—"

Skye blinked. She was lying on the floor. Nova was holding her, blood dripping from her wrists, magic still cracking like electricity in her fingertips.

"You're glowing," Skye murmured.

Nova gave a broken laugh. "Yeah. Just noticed."

Skye coughed. "That... that went wrong, right?"

Nova nodded. "Very wrong."

They sat like that for a while, the world spinning around them, the ritual smoldering in its half-finished state.

Skye turned her face into Nova's shoulder.

"I'm not just scared of dying," she whispered. "I'm scared that I'll die and no one will remember me. That I'll just... vanish. Like all the other Chosen. Like Isolde."

Nova's arms tightened around her.

"I would remember," she said. "Even if the whole town forgot. I'd carve your name into the moon if I had to."

Skye laughed, broken and breathless. "You'd curse the moon, probably."

"Only a little," Nova said. "And only if you asked."

LATER, when the witches helped them up, one of them pointed to the stone basin.

A mark had been left behind in the blood—a spiral of flame and thorns.

"It wasn't a binding," the elder said softly. "It was a **warning**."

Skye stared at the mark, her hand still wrapped in bandages.

The Moon wasn't just watching.

It was **coming.**

8

THREADS OF THE MOON

The Blood Moon rose before the sun set.
   It wasn't just earlier than expected—it was **wrong**.
Skye stared at the sky from her window, heart hammering as daylight bled into red. It wasn't a trick of the clouds. The Moon was there, **visible in the daylight**, swollen and red, perched low like it had crept in uninvited.
   She grabbed her journal and jotted the time: **4:36 PM.**
   Then she blinked.
   The sky was dark.
   Her clock read **1:03 AM.**
   She gasped, stumbled back from the window, blinking rapidly.
   And just like that, it was 4:36 again.
   She looked down.
   The ink in her journal was still wet.

AT FIRST, she thought it was exhaustion. Hallucinations. After all, she hadn't truly slept since the failed binding. Her nights were a carousel of fragmented dreams, her thoughts drifting like ash caught on the wind. But then came the mirror.

She passed it in the hallway—her grandmother's old heirloom, carved with ravens—and something made her stop.

Her reflection didn't move.

It stared back, blinking slower than her own eyes, a delay like a faulty film reel. Then, slowly, it smiled.

Skye hadn't.

She touched the mirror. Her reflection didn't.

Instead, it leaned forward and whispered in a voice that didn't come from the glass—but from **inside her skull**:

"You're already gone, Skye."

SKYE TORE AWAY and ran to Nova's room, her knuckles pounding the door hard enough to sting.

Nova answered instantly, already dressed, eyes wild. "You're feeling it too, aren't you?"

Skye nodded, breath shaky. "Time's—wrong. It's skipping. It's like I'm seeing... versions of things that haven't happened. Or *already did*."

Nova didn't hesitate. "Get your boots. We're going to the Hollowing Wood. Now."

THE FOREST GREETED them like it had been waiting.

No wind. No birds. Just fog—dense and low, curling around the trees like vines made of breath. The moment they passed into the clearing, Skye felt it in her bones: **the veil was paper-thin here.**

Nova's eyes scanned the space. "There's another circle," she muttered. "It wasn't here before."

She was right.

Burned into the earth was a second, warped ritual ring—like the one they'd cast before, but distorted, as if done by an unsteady hand or **under duress**. At the center, a handprint still smoldered into the dirt.

Skye knelt beside it.

Her hand fit perfectly.

A hum pulsed through her palm like a tuning fork.

Nova stepped back. "Don't—Skye—"

But it was too late.

The world fell away.

SHE BLINKED and found herself standing in the **town square**.

But it was wrong.

Everything was quiet. Too quiet.

Lanterns hung from ropes, swaying in a wind that didn't move the trees. The fountain was dry. The festival banners torn and fluttering like forgotten flags.

No voices. No music.

No life.

And then she saw **herself**.

Lying still on the altar.

Mouth parted, face pale. Her dress—the one she'd been told to wear for the ritual—was soaked in blood.

The crowd around her didn't move. They stared straight ahead, faces blank, eyes hollow. They looked carved from wax.

Elijah stood just behind her body. His expression unreadable.

Nova knelt at her side, her mouth open in a silent scream.

Then, through the stillness, something *shifted*.

The crowd parted without moving.

A figure emerged.

It had no face. No voice. Just a crown of bone and a cloak made of black smoke, its presence swallowing light.

The Blood Spirit.

It moved toward her body—her corpse—and knelt.

Skye tried to scream, to move, to intervene, but she was *watching*—a ghost in her own memory.

The spirit leaned down, and in a voice as old as dust and just as dry, it whispered:

"Belief fed me, but fear made me flesh."

Then it turned its head.

And **looked directly at her.**

"You've seen your death. Now choose: run or burn."

S<small>KYE FELL BACKWARD INTO HERSELF</small>.

Back in the clearing, she landed hard on her palms, gasping, trembling, soaked in sweat.

Nova rushed to her side. "You're back—you just *disappeared*. What did you see?"

Skye looked at her with wide, tear-filled eyes.

"I saw the ritual. I saw *me*, dead on the altar. And it—it whispered to me."

Nova's voice was hoarse. "What did it say?"

"That belief made it powerful, but *fear* gave it form."

Nova went still.

"So if we stop believing in the curse, if we stop being afraid of it..."

"We unmake it," Skye finished.

Then her voice dropped to a whisper. "But I think it knows."

She looked up at the sky.

The Moon was **huge now**, no longer red, but **bleeding black** at the edges.

Time was running out.

And this time, death wasn't coming for her.

It was **coming from her.**

9

HEART OF THE CURSE

The fire crackled low in the hearth, casting long, restless shadows across the worn floorboards of the Thorne house. Outside, fog clung to the windows like a second skin. It had been thick for days now, heavy with moisture and meaning, refusing to lift even in the pale hours of morning.

Skye sat cross-legged on the floor, the **grimoire** spread before her like a living thing. Its pages fluttered in an unfelt wind, ink rising and shifting across the parchment like breath across glass. The air around it hummed.

Nova crouched beside her, a candle cupped in her hand, the flame a trembling orb of gold. Her other hand held a pencil, dancing urgently across a growing map of notes and fragments, all copied from the journal, the catacombs, and Isolde's blood-written memories.

They had been at this for hours.

Skye's eyes were red from reading, her fingers ink-stained. Her hair hung in loose waves over her face, but she didn't notice. Not anymore. She was lost in the words—each one a breadcrumb in the dark.

Then, without warning, a line scrawled itself across the page.

The Chosen is not the sacrifice. She is the seal.
Skye's breath caught. Her voice broke the silence.
"Nova. Read this."
Nova leaned over, frowning as the words shifted again—blotting out, reforming into three jagged lines of script:
The Curse lives not by death, but by the consent of the dying.
The Moon feeds not on flesh, but on faith.
A willing soul seals the spell eternal.
They stared at it.
And then, in perfect unison:
"If I die willingly… I *become* the curse."

THE REALIZATION SETTLED between them like ash.

Nova stood first, pacing, eyes sharp with fury. "All this time, they weren't protecting us. They were trapping us. Building a lie so big even the victims believed it."

"They said I was chosen to *save* Hallow's End," Skye whispered, her voice hollow. "But I was chosen to *anchor* the curse. My death would give it permanence. It's not about appeasing the Blood Spirit—it's about feeding the town's fear. Their belief."

Nova slammed her notebook shut. "We have to tell them. We have to show them the truth."

Skye closed the grimoire gently, hands trembling. "It won't be enough."

Nova turned. "What?"

"They need to see it. Not just read it. **Feel it.**"

Nova tilted her head, understanding beginning to bloom like a dangerous flower. "You mean… you're going to walk into your own ritual."

"And I'm going to stop it."

NIGHT HAD FALLEN hard by the time the knock came.

Three short raps. Hesitant. Familiar.

Nova stiffened, reaching for her blade, but Skye had already crossed the room. Her hand hovered above the handle. She didn't know why she opened the door—only that part of her had already guessed who stood behind it.

And she was right.

Elijah.

He looked thinner than she remembered. Dark circles pooled beneath his eyes, and the cloak he wore hung too loose, like it no longer belonged to him.

"Skye," he said softly.

She didn't speak.

"I know I don't have the right to be here," he said, stepping into the light. "But I need to show you something. Something only the Watchers know."

Skye narrowed her eyes. "You mean the people planning to kill me?"

Elijah flinched. "Yes. And I'm not pretending I haven't failed you. I did. I believed the stories. I believed that sacrifice was the only way. But you showed me something else."

Skye said nothing. But she let him in.

The fire crackled again. Nova stood with her arms folded, watching Elijah like a storm about to strike.

He reached into his coat and pulled out a scroll. Old. Stamped in wax with the crest of the First Council—five sigils arranged in a circle.

"This is the original Rite," he said. "The one they use every hundred years."

He unrolled it carefully, pointing to the final lines.

Let the Chosen come with will, and the Moon shall bind the veil anew. The offering must not fight, or the pact shall weaken.

Nova's voice was a knife. "So it was always a choice. A lie wrapped in pageantry."

Elijah nodded. "But the Watchers knew the truth. We're taught to convince the Chosen. Gently, if possible. Forcefully, if not."

"And what happens," Skye asked slowly, "if the Chosen *refuses* the altar... in front of the town?"

Elijah looked at her. "The curse begins to unravel. The Spirit wakes. Chaos follows."

Skye sat back.

There it was.

Her death would save the town, but only for another century. Her survival—**her refusal**—would burn the whole lie to the ground.

LATER, after Elijah left, Nova sat with her in the dark.

Neither spoke.

Then Skye whispered, "I don't know if I'm strong enough."

Nova turned to her. "You're not. Not alone. But that's the point. You don't have to be."

She reached out, took Skye's hand.

"You're not the seal, Skye. You're the match."

OUTSIDE, the Moon swelled brighter. Too bright.

It was coming. And so were they.

But so was **Skye.**

And this time, she wasn't the Chosen.

She was the Reckoning.

10

THE PLAN

The town square had never looked more beautiful. Strings of lanterns floated above the cobbled streets like captured stars, their flames flickering gold and crimson. Masked dancers twirled to the hollow beat of old drums, and vendors handed out cider, sugared apples, and cloves strung like charms.

It was the final night of the Harvest Festival.

The **Night of the Offering.**

And the Blood Moon—bloated and pulsing with light—loomed impossibly close, like it had descended from the sky to witness the ancient pact with its own gleaming eye.

But beneath the laughter, beneath the music and tradition, something trembled.

A thread pulled taut.

Skye could feel it in her bones.

Tonight, everything would break.

SHE STOOD with Nova and Elijah beneath the bell tower of the old chapel, just out of sight of the main stage. The town's Elders moved like rooks across a chessboard, robed in shadow, whispering ancient blessings into the hands of townspeople who never questioned their rituals.

Nova unrolled the final page of the grimoire—the spell that would tear open the veil.

"It's all here," she whispered. "The memory anchor. The flame conjuration. The blood seal. We can project it—Isolde's truth—across the entire square. But it has to be done in the exact center."

"Where they'll kill me," Skye said softly.

Elijah stepped forward, his voice low. "You won't die. I swear it."

She looked at him. "I don't need promises. I need you to **hold the circle.**"

He nodded, solemn.

Nova pulled the small vial of Isolde's preserved blood—taken from the catacomb altar, wrapped in runes and sealed with moonstone.

"This is our match," she said. "Skye is the flame."

THEY MOVED like shadows through the crowd, cloaked by distraction, by masks and music. When Skye stepped onto the dais, heads began to turn. Some cheered. Some cried. Some looked away, unable to face the weight of tradition.

She saw her mother.

Her father.

Neither of them smiled.

Mayor Elswith stepped forward, her hands clasped tight around the ceremonial scroll.

"On this sacred night," she began, voice ringing with ritual, "we honor the pact that has kept our town safe—"

"No," Skye said.

The word cut like glass.

Elswith blinked.

Skye stepped fully into the light. Her voice rose, trembling but strong.

"We've honored a lie. We've fed our children to a spirit born not of protection—but of **fear.**"

Gasps echoed.

She reached into her cloak and pulled out the grimoire. Opened it to the blood-marked page.

"This is Isolde Thorne's truth. The one you buried. The one you burned."

Nova stepped beside her, drawing a line of fire in the air with her blade, murmuring the spell.

Elijah stood opposite, pressing his hands to the earth, anchoring the projection.

The magic swelled.

And then—**light**.

The square trembled as the sky above them **split**.

Flames burst upward in a spiral. A great shimmer unfolded from the center of the circle, wrapping around the crowd in a dome of light and sound.

And then—**a memory**.

Projected in the air like a vision:

Isolde, bound in chains, her eyes blazing.

"You call this protection?" she screamed. "You trade your daughters for calm seas. Your sons for quiet winters. This is not peace. This is cowardice."

"The Moon does not save you. It feeds on you."

The crowd watched, stunned, silent.

Isolde turned slowly, her spirit burning in the light.

"End it. Not by blade or spell. But by truth. Tear out the root of the lie, and the tree will fall."

The projection faded.

Smoke curled into the sky.

And the Moon pulsed—once—hard enough to make the ground quake.

Skye stepped to the edge of the altar. Her voice, now a whisper across the crowd:

"You were never saved. You were silenced."

And then she turned to the Elders.
"I will not die for your peace."
She stepped **down** from the altar.
The crowd exhaled as one.
The ritual had been broken.
But so had the seal.

THE MOON TURNED DARKER. The wind screamed.
And from the shadows, something ancient stirred.
The Blood Spirit had awakened.
But so had the town.
And this time, they were watching.
Not with belief.
Not with fear.
But with **truth**.

PART III

BLOOD MOON RISING

11

HALLOWEEN

The streets of **Hallow's End** glowed like a haunted painting. Lanterns swung from every rooftop, their candlelit bellies casting flickering shadows that stretched and shrank like breathing. The wind curled through the cobblestones, stirring cloaks and silks and skeletal lace.

Children wore paper-mâché fox masks. Teens in hollow-eyed skull paint lounged near vendors selling cloves and black sugar. The scent of cider, firewood, and something sharper—something coppery—thickened the air.

Every window bore a candle.
Every door, a chalk-drawn ward.
Every person wore a mask.
Because it was **Sacrifice Night**.
That was the way.

SKYE WALKED SLOWLY through the main avenue, flanked by Nova and Elijah. Their hoods were up, faces mostly hidden, though many townsfolk parted quietly as they passed—half reverent, half afraid.

The air felt thinner.

The Moon—**the Blood Moon**—was massive above them now, swollen to an unnatural size. It wasn't just red anymore. It was the color of flame behind flesh, of fresh bruises and dried roses. It filled the sky like an open eye.

Nova whispered, "It's too early. It wasn't supposed to rise until midnight."

Skye nodded without answering.

She felt it. That pressure. Like the Moon had bent gravity itself, and her body was no longer her own. Her blood pulsed harder. Her breath came slower.

The ritual was broken—but **the Moon still wanted a soul.**

THEY REACHED the square just before the clock struck eleven.

It had been transformed.

The altar had been raised again—draped in black silk, surrounded by white lilies and bone-white lanterns. Five robed Elders stood behind it, their masks stitched with ancient sigils in silver thread.

Wind tore down the avenue like a scream. Somewhere, a bell rang once. Twice.

Skye stepped forward alone.

Every step felt like a choice. A defiance.

Behind her, Nova murmured a soft spell for protection. Elijah placed his hand to the earth, anchoring the ritual beneath the altar to weaken the Moon's influence.

They were ready.

Skye reached the steps of the platform.

Mayor Elswith stood above, her face half-shrouded, hands clutching the ceremonial scroll like a shield.

"You come of your own will?" she asked, the words brittle.

Skye raised her head. "No."

A murmur moved through the crowd.

"I come to end this. Not to fulfill it."

She turned to face the town.

"Tonight is not about peace. Or sacrifice. It's about **control**. It's about fear."

Lightning cracked in the distance. The wind howled again.

And then—without warning—all the lanterns **blew out.**

The Moon surged in the sky.

And from the darkness behind the altar, something began to rise.

A SCREAM CUT through the silence.

It was not human.

It was a thousand voices folded into one—a sound that peeled at the edges of reality.

The Blood Spirit.

It unfolded from the altar's shadow like smoke turned to bone, its face hidden by a mask made of curved antlers and ash. It was tall, towering, its limbs too long, its presence warping the light around it.

Skye stared into the hollow where its eyes should be.

And it spoke.

Not with words, but with **memory**.

She saw herself as a child, standing in a field of dead trees.

Her grandmother's voice whispering lullabies that were actually spells.

Her name being called from a scroll—again, and again, and again.

Then the voice came.

"You have broken the seal. But one must still fall."

The crowd dropped to their knees.

Elijah stepped forward. "She won't."

Nova flanked Skye, flames dancing along her fingers.

And Skye—Skye looked up at the Spirit and said, voice ringing with defiance:

"Then take me. But I won't go quietly. I won't go believing. I won't go in fear."

The Moon pulsed. The altar cracked.

And the Spirit **screamed.**

12

TRUTH UNDONE

The altar groaned beneath Skye's boots as she stepped fully into the circle.

The Blood Spirit towered behind her, a god-shaped shadow stretching across the stage, its antlered crown haloed by the swollen red Moon. The wind screamed through the square, slashing at cloaks, extinguishing candles, rattling bones strung like wind chimes.

The crowd knelt in silence, held captive not by reverence, but by **terror**.

This was not ceremony anymore.

It was reckoning.

Nova took her place just behind Skye, gripping the grimoire tight to her chest. Her mouth moved in silent prayer—not to the Moon, but to Isolde. To memory. To magic.

The final spell was stitched across three pages, written in blood and secrecy. It wasn't a weapon.

It was a *confession*.

Nova struck the flint.

A ring of flame burst into life around the platform—casting a warm, golden light that cut through the Moon's red haze.

And then she began the incantation.

Her voice rose above the wind, steady, sure:

"Blood of the betrayed. Voice of the silenced. Let truth rise like smoke and memory."

"Let her speak."

"Let them see."

THE FLAMES PULSED.

The air shimmered.

And Isolde Thorne appeared.

Not in flesh—but in **memory made light.**

The illusion spiraled above the platform, woven from magic and grief. A ghost rendered in gold and fire.

Her face was streaked with ash, her hair a storm of tangled black. Her wrists were bound in ceremonial chains, and her mouth moved before her voice was heard.

"YOU KNOW MY NAME."

"You have buried it beneath centuries of lies."

"But I have always been watching."

THE CROWD GASPED.

Elder Rowan staggered backward.

Isolde turned, her projection facing the people of Hallow's End.

"I was the Fifth. The one who said no."

"They called me a traitor. A heretic. But I was a mother. A sister. A witch who saw the truth too clearly to stay silent."

The illusion shifted.

Now she stood in a forest clearing—her final night.

"They said the Blood Moon demanded a soul. But the Moon does not think. The Moon does not want."

"**You wanted.** You feared. And so it fed."

The image darkened.

A cloaked figure stepped forward in the illusion—Elijah's great-grandfather.

He drove the blade into her heart.

THE SQUARE HELD ITS BREATH.

Somewhere, a child began to cry.

ISOLDE TURNED ONCE MORE, her voice now thunder:

"A curse does not live in the sky."

"It lives in your silence. In your fear. In the story you choose to pass down, instead of the one that actually happened."

"You do not need to be saved. You need to **wake up.**"

THE ILLUSION SHATTERED into ash and light.

The flames collapsed. The wind died.

And for the first time in centuries, **the crowd did not kneel.**

They stood.

They looked at each other, confused, shaken, blinking at a history they had never been allowed to see.

A woman near the back pulled off her mask and whispered, "My grandmother told me stories of Isolde. Said she had fire in her blood. I thought they were bedtime tales."

A man beside her murmured, "She was real."

Another: "They lied to us."

And slowly—like a dam cracking beneath water—**the belief began to break.**

📜 Isolde Thorne's Final Diary Entry

October 31st, 1925

They think a curse is a thing you place. A word you whisper. A knife you bury.

But curses are belief made solid. Fear made law. A story told again and again until it grows teeth.

They called me dangerous. And I was.

Because I told them the truth: that no Moon, no god, no spirit has power unless we hand it over with both shaking hands.

I was not sacrificed.

I was **silenced**.

But I have waited.

And now—**I am heard.**

Skye stepped down from the altar, not as a lamb to slaughter—

But as a **spark**.

The crowd parted for her. No longer because they feared her death.

But because, finally, they understood she had chosen **life**.

13

ONE MUST DIE

For a breathless moment, everything was still.

The wind, the crowd, the stars—all paused like the world had exhaled and forgotten how to breathe again.

But the Moon remembered.

It pulsed in the sky like a wound trying to close.

The Blood Spirit—still towering behind the cracked altar—screamed in silence, its form distorting, collapsing in on itself and blooming outward again. No longer fully tethered, it flickered like a candle near extinction.

But it wasn't gone.

It was *hungry*.

And above them, the Moon flared once—then **burned.**

Crimson light poured down, drowning the square in color. The crowd staggered back, some crying out. Children clung to their mothers. The Elders tried to speak, but their words were devoured by the wind.

A voice, not spoken but **felt**, moved through the square.

"The story is broken. But the pact is not."

"One must die."

. . .

SKYE FELT it in her chest first—a pull, gentle and persistent, like a thread tugging her forward. Her blood hummed. The mark on her hand burned with heat.

She stepped toward the altar again, the crowd parting silently as she moved.

Nova shouted something, but it was distant—like sound underwater.

Skye looked up at the Moon. It was no longer a symbol. No longer a myth.

It was **sentient**.

It wanted balance.

She stepped into the circle of ash and flame, eyes lifted, shoulders squared.

"I'll do it," she whispered. "You want a soul? Take mine."

The Blood Spirit leaned forward, its form folding like smoke around her. The shadows brushed her cheek like breath. Her skin burned where they touched.

Then—just as she reached the altar—

Hands caught her from behind.

Elijah.

He spun her around and shoved her back—**hard**—so she landed outside the circle, gasping. Her body jolted. The magic didn't reach her there.

"Elijah, no—!" Skye screamed, scrambling up.

But he was already stepping into her place.

The shadows accepted him like they'd been waiting all along.

His voice, quiet and sure, found her through the chaos:

"You showed me I could choose."

"Let this be mine."

She ran forward—but Nova grabbed her, arms locked tight around her ribs.

"He made the choice, Skye," Nova whispered, breaking.

Tears streamed down Skye's cheeks, mixing with ash.

"Elijah!"

But he didn't look back.

The Blood Spirit wrapped itself around him, and for a moment—just a flicker—Elijah **glowed**. Not with pain.

But with **peace**.

He mouthed something to her, and though the wind howled and the world trembled, she heard it like a secret whispered in a dream:

"Live free."

Then the light exploded.

The Moon screamed.

And the Spirit—**shattered.**

It didn't burn.

It *unmade*.

The light collapsed inward, tearing the shadows with it, like a great inhale pulling everything that had ever been feared back into the void it came from.

And then—

Silence.

THE MOON DIMMED.

Its blood-red hue faded to pale silver.

The altar cracked in two.

And the town stood in stunned stillness beneath a sky that, for the first time in a hundred years, **belonged only to the stars.**

Skye fell to her knees, sobbing.

Not from guilt.

Not from defeat.

But because **it was over**.

NOVA KNELT BESIDE HER, arms wrapped around her like roots around a buried seed.

Together, they wept.

For Elijah.

For Isolde.
For every Chosen who had never known the freedom of refusal.

LATER, someone would write it down.
Someone would ask how it ended.
And Skye would answer: "**With a choice.**"

14

THE MOURNING LIGHT

By the time the wind stopped howling, the world had changed.

Skye sat on the cold stone steps of the broken altar, her palms flat against the worn surface, grounding herself to something—anything—that still felt real.

The square was empty now.

Lanterns hung from broken ropes, their candles long since snuffed. Banners trailed like loose threads. The wind no longer roared. It whispered, brushing the blood-dusted ground with gentle fingers.

The **Blood Moon**, so huge and consuming only hours ago, had faded with the stars. It hung in the sky now as a pale sliver—fragile and shrinking, as if the night itself had exhaled and let it go.

And Skye?

She didn't cry.

Not yet.

Her grief sat inside her like coals—**hot, glowing, but contained.**

THE TOWNSPEOPLE HAD DRIFTED AWAY after the Spirit vanished.

Some had fled.
Others stayed behind longer, frozen, staring at the altar as if trying to decipher whether what they had witnessed had been **real** or some fever-dream spell.

Nova had gone with the remaining witches, promising to return.

"Let them see us now," she'd said. "Not in the shadows. In the sun."

Skye had only nodded.

She needed this moment alone.

A SMALL CLUSTER of white lilies lay beside her—the ones that had been scattered around the altar before the ritual.

She picked one up and turned it slowly in her fingers.

The petals were wilting now. Softening.

How many sacrifices had stood where she now sat? How many names buried beneath centuries of ceremony, scrubbed clean of memory, honored only in empty tradition?

But not Elijah.

Not him.

She wouldn't let that happen.

THE MEMORY CAME FAST and hard:

His hand against her shoulder.

The way he stepped into her place, not as a martyr, but as a man finally free to choose something that mattered.

"You showed me I could choose."

She pressed her forehead against her knees and finally let the tears fall.

Not out of guilt.

Not regret.

Just love. Real, human, *unfiltered* love. For a boy who had been born into silence and chose to **break it**.

. . .

She didn't hear them arrive.

She simply felt the **shift**—in the air, in the light, in the soft hush that suddenly surrounded her like prayer.

Skye looked up slowly.

And there they were.

They stood at the edge of the ruined square where fog met light— **Isolde and Elijah,** bathed in the gray-gold bloom of morning.

Neither ghost nor dream.

More than memory. Less than flesh.

Elijah looked... light. Not glowing. Just *unburdened*. His dark hair moved with the wind, and his eyes—those same soft, sharp eyes she'd known all her life—met hers without sorrow.

He smiled. Small. Familiar.

And Skye's chest ached with something sweet and sharp all at once.

Isolde stood beside him, a quiet force of flame and serenity. She wore a cloak of deep midnight, stitched with silver vines, her bare feet pale against the stones. Her presence held centuries. Her gaze held Skye.

And when she spoke, it wasn't with her mouth, but with something deeper.

"You did what I could not."

"You freed us."

Skye rose slowly, walking to the edge of the altar's platform, her breath catching in her throat.

"I was so scared," she said, voice hoarse. "Not of dying. Of *being forgotten*."

Elijah shook his head, gently.

"You won't be."

He looked over the square, at the cracked stone and the rising light, and then back at her.

"You changed the story."

A soft breeze curled around her ankles, brushing her skin like a goodbye.

Elijah took Isolde's hand.

The woman smiled, radiant and fierce.

Then they began to fade.

NOT ALL AT ONCE.

Like the Moon itself, they dimmed gradually, turning from people to silhouettes, then to outlines, then to light.

And then—gone.

Not erased.

Released.

THE SUN BREACHED THE HORIZON.

A new day. A real one.

Skye stood alone in the ruins of tradition, her hand resting over her heart.

She closed her eyes.

Breathed in deep.

When she opened them again, she turned not to the past—

But to the path Nova had carved through the fog, still fresh, leading forward.

SKYE DIDN'T KNOW what came next.

But she was no longer afraid of the unknown.

She was done surviving someone else's story.

Now she was ready to write her own.

15

KEEPER OF THE FLAME

It had been three months since the Blood Moon faded.

Three months since the altar cracked, the crowd broke, and the Spirit dissolved into shadow and ash.

And **Hallow's End**, once a place of old fear and soft lies, was waking up.

The town didn't change overnight. Some things clung stubbornly to the past—some people still lit candles on their doorsteps for "safety," and some Elders refused to speak Isolde's name. But the masks stayed tucked in drawers that Halloween. The scroll stayed sealed. The altar stayed buried in dust.

And no one—**not one soul**—knelt on Sacrifice Night.

SKYE SAT in the sunlight near the library steps, her back against a stone column, a leather-bound journal balanced on her knees. The cover was etched by hand, the title pressed in silver foil:

The Truth of Hallow's Eve

by Skye Amelia Mercer

She had filled three-fourths of it already.

Spells. Testimonies. Isolde's real words. Elijah's name. Her own memories, messy and raw. She wrote it not for power, not for pity—but for **remembrance**.

So that no girl would ever be told that fear was sacred again.

Nova had flourished in the light.

Where once she wore bone charms and shadows like armor, now she wore sunlit cloaks and led circles of children through the fields outside the chapel ruins, teaching them the **magic of protection,** of intuition, of choice.

"No blood magic," she always warned them with a grin. "Unless it's for an emergency."

They adored her.

And Skye adored them.

One afternoon, a little girl tugged at Skye's sleeve and whispered, "Are you the one who said no?"

Skye had smiled.

"Yeah," she said. "That was me."

On Halloween night—not **the Night of the Offering**, but Halloween, as it had once been and always should have been—Skye walked through the softened streets of Hallow's End alone.

Not in mourning.

In ritual.

She reached the edge of the woods and sat beneath the old yew tree, where the fog still kissed the grass, where memory still lingered, but fear no longer ruled.

She took a match from her coat pocket.

Lit a candle.

Set it down on the moss-covered stone in front of her.

It flickered once, then burned steady.

"For Elijah," she whispered.

She didn't cry.

She didn't need to.

He was part of the flame now.

Above her, the Moon hung low in the sky.
It was **silver** again.
Soft and watching.
But this time, **so was she**.
She tilted her head, narrowed her eyes, and whispered, almost smiling:
"I see you."
And then she turned back toward the path.

The moon was silver again—
but I still watched it.

End of Book One: Hallow's Eve: The Curse of the Blood Moon

AFTERWORD ON BREAKING THE CYCLE

By Aria Blake

When I first began writing *Hallow's Eve: The Curse of the Blood Moon*, I thought I was telling a story about witches, sacrifice, and small-town secrets.

But somewhere along the way, I realized I was writing about something much closer to home.

I was writing about fear.

About expectation.

About being told who you're supposed to be—before you even have a chance to decide for yourself.

This book is about **destiny versus choice**—about the moment you realize that the path laid out for you isn't the only one you can walk. That you can step off it. Burn it. Make your own.

In *Hallow's End*, Skye is told that her death is an honor. That tradition is sacred. That fear is necessary. And worst of all—that her fate was sealed before she was born.

Many of us know that feeling, even if we've never stood beneath a blood-red moon.

We feel it when we're told we can't change.

When we're told that history must be obeyed.

AFTERWORD ON BREAKING THE CYCLE

When we're told that silence is safer than speaking.
When we inherit pain disguised as pride.
But here's the truth:
You are allowed to question the stories you've been handed.
You are allowed to rewrite them.
And you are *absolutely allowed* to choose yourself.
Skye didn't break the curse with magic alone.
She broke it by saying **no**.
By facing fear without bowing to it.
By choosing a different ending—even when it cost her everything.
That power lives in all of us.

If you've ever felt like your path was chosen for you, I hope this book reminds you that it doesn't have to stay that way. The story can still change. You can still change it.

So write your own page.
Light your own candle.
And when someone says "This is just the way it's always been," ask them—
"But what if it doesn't have to be?"

With fire,

Aria Blake